Day Care

W9-CFF-576

A Giant First-Start Reader

This easy reader contains only 57 different words, repeated often to help the young reader develop word recognition and interest in reading.

Basic word list for *The Great Bunny Race*

a	front	runs
all	get	says
am	go	see
and	have	set
are	he	slow
as	hooray	so
Boomer	I	than
bunnies	if	the
bunny	in	they
but	is	to
can	must	Toby
Darby	no	tries
duck	of	try
even	others	wants
every	past	who
fast	race	win
faster	ready	wins
fastest	run	year
for	running	you

The
Great Bunny Race

Written by Kathy Feczko

Illustrated by John Jones

Troll Associates

Library of Congress Cataloging in Publication Data

Feczko, Kathy.
    The great bunny race.

    Summary: Can slow Toby outrun champion racer, Boomer
Bunny, at the Annual Rabbit Race?
        1. Children's stories, American. [1. Rabbits—Fiction.
2. Racing—Fiction] I. Jones, John, 1935-   ill.
II. Title.
PZ7.F2985Gr   1985   [E]   84-8634
ISBN 0-8167-0357-4 (lib. bdg.)

Copyright © 1985 by Troll Associates, Mahwah, New Jersey
All rights reserved. No part of this book may be used
or reproduced in any manner whatsoever without written
permission from the publisher.
Printed in the United States of America

10 9 8 7 6 5 4 3 2 1

Every year, the bunnies have a race.

They race to see who is the fastest of all.

And every year, Boomer Bunny wins.

"No bunny is faster than I," says Boomer.

Toby wants to win the race.

"But I am slow," says Toby.

"No bunny is faster than Boomer."

"But you must try," says Darby Duck.

"Try to see if you are faster than Boomer."

So Toby tries.

"Get ready!" says Darby Duck.

"Get set!" says Darby Duck.

"GO!" says Darby Duck.

And all the bunnies run.

Toby runs fast.

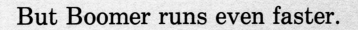
But Boomer runs even faster.

All the bunnies run and run and run.

"Go, Toby, go!" says Darby Duck.

"Go, go, go!"

Toby runs and runs.

He runs as fast as he can.

He runs past all the others.

He is running in front!

He is running faster than all the
others—even Boomer!

Toby is the fastest bunny of all!

Hooray for Toby! Hooray! Hooray!